Suddenly, from somewhere in front of Jack, a high-pitched cry, wild and shrill, pierced the early morning silence!

Jack froze and looked around. He couldn't see anything, but he could feel he wasn't alone. In spite of the cold, he began to sweat.

He stopped to listen a second time. There it was again, but this time the whine lasted a minute or more!

The hairs on the back of his neck stood up as he crept closer. . .

FLICK

ALSO BY LYNN FLOYD WRIGHT

The Prison Bird
Just One Blade
Flick The Hero!
Momma, Tell Me A Story
Daddy, Tell Me A Story

ALSO BY TONY WATERS

The Sailor's Bride
Just One Blade
Flick The Hero!

FLICK

written by
Lynn Floyd Wright

illustrated by
Tony Waters

WORRYWART PUBLISHING COMPANY
COLUMBIA

Requests for permission to make copies for any part of this work
should be mailed to:

Worrywart Publishing Company
337 White Birch Circle
Columbia, S.C. 29223

Production & Design: Janyce Collins, Design Plus!

Printed in the United States of America

3 5 7 9 10 8 6 4

Library of Congress Cataloging-in Publication Data

Wright, Lynn Floyd, 1957-
    Flick / written by Lynn Floyd Wright; illustrated by Tony Waters.
    p.   cm.
    Summary: Nine-year-old Jack finds a badly injured dog,
and even though his veterinarian father thinks the dog will not
survive, Jack is sure that it will.
    ISBN 1-881519-02-3 (hard: alk. paper)
    ISBN 1-881519-03-1 (paper: alk. paper)
    [1.Dogs — Fiction. 2. Fathers and sons — Fiction.]
I. Waters, Tony, 1958-   ill.   II. Title.
PZ7.W9565Fl   1995
[Fic] — dc20

                                              95-17842
                                                 CIP
                                                  AC

MICKEY GARRISON

To Skipper, my first best friend, with love always

~LFW~

*In memory of my Grandfather, Daddy Stumpy, who
was another spirited fighter*

~TW~

CHAPTER 1

"If Mom and Dad find out, we're gonna get it for sure. Jack! Are you listening to me?"

"Jack!"

Emily's warning was falling on deaf ears. Jack Coleman wasn't in the mood to listen to advice from anyone.

Especially from a girl. Or worse, a sister.

Emily ran to catch up with him. "Did you hear me, Jack? We're going to be late. Mrs. Johnson said if I'm late one more time, she'd call home. Then *you'll* really get it."

Jack ignored her and walked faster. Just what he needed today. Girls were bad enough, but little sisters were the pits. She could go on, but he had something better to do first.

It was almost his favorite time of day. The sun wasn't up yet, so everything up and down their street was still coated in gray. Another half hour and the gray would turn to gold, then pink.

Even the chill of the November air didn't bother him. The cold drizzle that had been with them the past five days had finally stopped last night and today promised to be the first sunny day of the month.

In Lancaster, South Carolina, winter was never too bad anyway. There was just enough snow to close school a few times without having to make up the days in the summer. In fact, except for a few weeks every year, the weather was good year round.

Good enough for fishing anyway. Which was why he had to go to the pond. He hadn't been all week.

And before the sky was that excellent shade of pink, Jack intended to be at his favorite place at his favorite time of day. If he hurried, he could just make it.

"Go on then," he yelled over his shoulder as he moved faster. "Who wants you tagging along anyway? I'm just going to check my bait trap, for crying out loud."

He stopped and turned around. "So go on, I said. I'll be

along. And I *won't* be late either."

Emily gave him a hurt look, then glared. "You and your stupid fish," she said and stamped off.

CHAPTER 2

Jack watched her go. He turned back and headed in the opposite direction, crossing two streets before coming to the road that led to the railroad yards. In front of him, two sets of railroad tracks — one belonging to the Norfolk-Southern, the other to the Lancaster and Chester — ran side by side.

He crossed over the first set of Norfolk-Southern tracks, turned right and began walking down the tracks belonging to the Lancaster and Chester. He loved to walk on the track this time of day. He knew the train schedules by heart; another train wasn't due for an hour. Plenty of time.

It was only a ten-minute walk down the track until he came to the path in the woods that led down to his pond. His pond— Coleman's Pond— was just on the other side of the woods.

Actually it wasn't his pond at all, but he liked to pretend it was. A few years ago, he and his dad had met the people who owned the property and they said he could use it anytime.

As he walked along the rails, his hightops made a soft padding noise and his jacket rustled against his flannel shirt.

The fish should be bitin' today, he thought as he got closer to the clearing in the woods. *I'll go this afternoon, right after...*

Suddenly Jack was distracted by something. When he was about a good stone's throw away from the path he heard a very strange noise.

It was a high-pitched cry, wild and shrill, and it seemed to be coming from somewhere in front of him!

Jack froze and looked around. He couldn't see anything nearby. The railroad yard was deserted. Even the men who unloaded the big coal cars that came in every morning were nowhere around. In spite of the cold, he began to sweat.

He stopped to listen a second time. There it was again! This time the whine lasted a minute or more.

The hairs on the back of his neck stood up as he crept closer.

CHAPTER 3

Jack edged forward, keeping low to the ground. He remembered what his father had always told him about being alone out here. There were plenty of animals living all through the woods surrounding his pond, but most were never brave enough to come out during the daylight hours. Which meant that whatever kind of animal it was, it was probably hurt.

Dad had always told him that a hurt animal doesn't know a friend from an enemy and could be very dangerous. And of all people his dad, *Doctor* Mike Coleman, ought to know because he was a veterinarian.

The whine came again. Jack moved a little closer. It was still a little too dark to see anything but shadows. But in the growing light, he thought he could see a small dark clump ahead on the railroad track.

A baby wolf? he thought. His heart raced at the thought. He had seen one at his father's clinic one time and had wanted one ever since.

Jack kept moving forward slowly, ready to turn and run

at the first sign of trouble. His heart was pounding so hard that he could feel his shirt jump with each beat.

So far, the little clump still hadn't moved. It just kept crying.

Jack was almost there, so close he could almost reach out and touch whatever it was. He took a deep breath and leaned forward to get a better look. He couldn't believe what he saw.

It wasn't a wolf. Or a fox. Or even a raccoon.

It was a dog! And it was lying — no, it was wedged down — between the tracks!

It had been run over by the train!

CHAPTER 4

Jack bent over the dog slowly. It was hard to tell what kind of dog it was because the body was smashed down so far between the rails.

It was lying on its right side. The body was about a foot long and had a stumpy little tail. It lay perfectly still.

Its head had a medium-size muzzle and short, floppy ears that hung down only an inch or so. A thin piece of cloth circled its small neck. The dark brown eyes, opened wide with fright, could barely be seen above the rim of the rail.

But it was the legs that Jack stared at. Two of them were all twisted up. They reminded Jack of mashed-up tin foil.

A thick mixture of dark red blood and black soot covered the little animal.

Jack turned quickly away and felt queasiness forcing its way up into his throat. He ran to the edge of the woods and threw up.

When his shaking stopped, he wiped his mouth with the sleeve of his jacket and took a deep breath. Before he could change his mind, he forced himself to go back for another look.

He noticed that the dog still hadn't moved. But now its eyes were closed.

"Hey fella," Jack said softly. There was no response.

"Puppy, can you hear me?" he asked a little louder. "Look at me, boy. Open your eyes. Do anything. Please."

The dog still didn't move. Even its whimpering had stopped.

He felt like crying. He was too late.

Jack started to turn away. Just as he did, something caught his eye. He wheeled around and said once more, "Pup?"

There it was again! He did see something! The little tail had moved! It was just a small movement, but it had just enough force to make a very tiny tap on the rail.

The dog was still alive!

CHAPTER 5

Jack's relief was so strong that for a minute he was frozen in place.

When his shock wore off, he squatted down beside the dog to think.

"Don't worry fella," he said, "I'll help you." He took off his jacket and laid it over the little dog. Its small brown eyes opened for a second and looked at him.

Jack's mind raced. What should he do? Run for help? Try to pull the dog out himself? Go find one of the railroad workers? His mind jumped from one plan to the next.

Then suddenly he knew. Of course! He should have thought of that first!

"They'll help. They'll know what to do," he reassured the little bundle. "Hang on boy. We'll get you out. I'll fix everything. Just hang on!"

Leaving his jacket wrapped around the dog and ignoring the cold, Jack got quickly to his feet.

Spinning around, he started back in the direction he had just come from.

His destination: the L & C Railway.

CHAPTER 6

The offices of the Lancaster and Chester Railway —
the L & C everyone in town called them — could be
found inside a brown and cream colored stone and brick
two-story building that was almost 100 years old.

Their trains ran east to west across upper South
Carolina and traveled over 29 miles of track from
Chester to Lancaster, stopping several times along the
way. Every day their cars brought coal and other materi-
als to the businesses on their route.

Jack stopped at the dark brown front door marked
General Office to catch his breath and check his watch.
Clifford Washington, "Mr. Cliff," should just be coming
on duty as he did at 8 o' clock every weekday morning.

Clifford Washington, the day stationmaster, had
worked for the L & C Railroad for 34 years.

A distinguished-looking black man with solid white
hair and a bushy moustache, he could rattle off every
train schedule, past and present, from all of those 34
years. Mr. Cliff's father and grandfather had all been rail-

road men; in all, three generations of Washingtons had proudly served the L & C Railroad. Everyone in town knew and loved them.

The children had special reason to love Mr. Cliff. Every year he set aside a day in June, on the last day of school, and took every first grader in Lancaster on a special train trip.

Jack had taken that train ride several years ago. He had been crazy about trains and Mr. Cliff ever since.

Jack found him inside his cluttered office, talking on the phone. "Mr. Cliff!" Jack blurted out a little louder than he meant to, ignoring the fact that the stationmaster was deep in conversation.

Mr. Cliff looked up harshly, then softened when he saw Jack's face.

"I'll get back to you," he said into the phone. "Jack, you're as red as a beet. Sit down boy and catch your breath. Then you can tell me what's the matter."

Jack sat down in the chair beside the desk. He took a few deep breaths, then told about his discovery.

"That sounds like the track for the 17 Eastbound," Washington said thoughtfully, patting down his moustache with his fingers. "Jack, that train runs through every two hours. You *sure* that dog was alive?"

Jack nodded. "I even saw his tail wag. That's how I knew. Please Mr. Cliff we've got to help it before it's too late!"

Mr. Cliff thought a minute. "Tell you what. Let me get someone to answer my phone and we'll go have a look. But first you call your dad and tell him what's happened. I'll make sure the train doesn't run on that track until the dog is moved."

Jack went into the next door office and called his father's office. The clinic wasn't open yet so he had to leave a message with his dad's answering service.

He went back to Mr. Cliff's office just in time to see the stationmaster reach inside his desk drawer and pull out a pistol.

Jack looked at him in horror. "Mr. Cliff, you can't! You just can't!"

Mr. Cliff's jaw was set in a straight line. "Jack, son I hope I don't have to. But if that dog's too far gone and really suffering, it's the only decent thing I can do. Now, let's go."

CHAPTER 7

The walk back was much too slow for Jack's taste. Mr. Cliff's legs were no match for Jack's and it took a bit longer than before to reach the track.

"Well, I'll be..." Mr. Cliff began as he knelt down by the still figure.

He removed Jack's coat and bent over to touch the dog's head, then reached down a little farther to find the neck. The pulse was very weak and barely noticeable. The dog whimpered and Jack felt himself getting queasy all over again.

Mr. Cliff didn't say anything for a few minutes. Then he turned to Jack and said quietly, "Jack, I don't think we can do anything for this poor thing but put it out of its misery. It's just beyond help."

Tears sprang to Jack's eyes and he swallowed hard. His stomach churned again and his feet felt like lead. He started to protest but the look from Mr. Cliff left him speechless.

"Why don't you start on out for school, son? I'll take care of everything. There's really no point in you staying around. It'll only get you more upset."

"I'll see it finished. I found him," was all Jack could manage to say.

As he watched, the stationmaster raised up his gun and took aim at the center of the dog's head, between the eyes. Jack closed his eyes. He heard the snap of the trigger as it was pulled back. He balled his hands into tight fists and waited.

Waited.

Waited.

Then...a click.

• • • • • • • • • • • • • • • • •

Jack opened his eyes and saw Mr. Cliff looking at the gun in disbelief.

"What in the world?" he muttered. "I just fired this thing last week and it worked fine." He checked the chamber to be sure it was fully loaded, then cocked the pistol a second time.

Jack wanted to say something but he was too surprised. Instead, he stared at the dog.

And that's when he saw it.

"Look!" Jack cried, finding his voice again. "Look quick!"

The stubby tail flipped from side to side once again! "You see! You can't shoot it! You can't!"

The stationmaster lowered his gun and nodded. "Let's go back and try your dad again," he said.

CHAPTER 8

Dr. Mike Coleman's veterinary office was located on the other side of Lancaster, just outside the city limits on Highway 9. A "Welcome to Lancaster - The Red Rose City" billboard was posted just beyond the long circular driveway out in front.

The building itself was a one-story orange brick building with a Lancaster Animal Clinic sign hanging to the right of the front door. A large picture window was just to the left.

Mike Coleman had been curing his "patients"— dogs, cats, rabbits, cows, horses, even an occasional wolf or fox— for the past ten years. He also served Lancaster county as Director of Animal Services. Five people, including a secretary, two part-time assistants and a lab technician, made up his staff.

The secretary, Laura Collins, picked up on the second ring. "Hello Jack," she said warmly.

Jack's words tumbled out in a rush. "I need to talk to my dad. I found a dog. It's hurt. Get him quick please."

"I'm sorry Jack," she apologized, "but your dad is over in Richburg today doing surgery. I expect he'll be away most of the day, til late afternoon at the earliest."

Jack smacked his forehead with the palm of his hand. He knew that every Friday his dad went to Richburg. In all the excitement, he forgot. "But I need him," he wailed, feeling ashamed at his whining. "You've just got to call him."

"Tell you what," Mrs. Collins said. "I'll call over there and leave a message for him to call me as soon as he can. Now, tell me where you are."

CHAPTER 9

Mr. Cliff called Jack's mom, then sent him on to school with a promise to get word to him if his dad arrived before the end of classes.

But Jack couldn't concentrate on any school work. He was worried sick. Twice he went to the office to call his dad, but still couldn't reach him.

So he just stared off into space, watched the clock and thought about the dog.

The dog. His dog. This was the one. He was sure of it. It was meant to be his. He'd been begging for a dog all year, but the rule was he couldn't have one until he was twelve and that was still too far away.

Yet it seemed that everyone in his family had a pet but him. His mother had two tabby cats, Fric and Frac, that slept all day. *Useless.*

Emily had some goldfish, Peter and Fred, in a bowl in her room. *Boring.*

Even his dad had the old hound dog General but he stayed at his office. *Unfamiliar.*

He wanted something that would belong to just him. He wanted a dog. *This dog.*

His thoughts were interrupted when the bell rang. He raced out of the building without waiting to walk Emily home.

CHAPTER 10

Jack arrived at the railway offices to find no change. Clifford Washington was in his office. "Come on in Jack," the stationmaster said. "Your dad called just a minute ago. He's on his way." Then, as if he knew Jack's next question added, "and the last time I checked, your little friend was still with us."

Jack sighed with relief. "I'll be outside."

At almost 4 o' clock, Mike Coleman's old Cherokee clattered into the L & C parking lot. Jack looked up from his place beside the dog when he heard the familiar white Jeep.

As Dr. Coleman got out with his medical bag in hand, Jack ran to meet him. Even from a distance, anyone could tell that Mike and Jack Coleman were father and son. Both were tall and thin and had the same color dark red hair and green eyes. They even walked the same way, taking long strides as if they were in a hurry.

"Sorry it took me so long to get here son," he said. "I finally got your message."

Jack started to explain. "Dad, you've just got to help it. You can...I know..." His words were coming out so fast, he knew he wasn't making any sense at all.

Clifford Washington caught up with them and explained. "Jack found it this morning Mike," he said as the two men shook hands. "It's pretty far gone I think. I tried to put it out of its misery this morning but my gun wouldn't fire. Before I could try again, it moved. I just didn't have the heart to try again."

Dr. Coleman bent down for a closer look. "Easy fella. I just want to look." The dog didn't move.

"Mike, for what it's worth, this is the track that the 17 Eastbound comes in on every two hours, so I don't know how many times it's been hit or how long it's been here."

Dr. Coleman listened but didn't say anything. He frowned all the time his fingers were moving up and down the small body.

Finally he looked at Jack. "Son, there's nothing I can do. I've got to put it down."

Jack felt faint. His disappointment at trying so hard

only to have his father give up so quickly was too much to bear.

He choked back a sob and then began to cry. His father held him tightly. "I'm sorry," he said softly. "I can't let it keep suffering."

He turned away to reach into his little black bag for a syringe and the bottle of painkiller.

Mr. Cliff walked up to guide Jack away. Jack jerked away angrily. "It's not fair. I WANT HIM!" he screamed.

At the sound of his voice, the dog slightly raised his head.

"Dad, look!"

Dr. Coleman's eyes followed Jack's finger. His eyebrows lifted in surprise.

"You see it too?" Mr. Cliff asked in a shaky voice. "It's not my imagination, right?"

"Yes, and I don't believe it," Mike Coleman answered. "How could it even have the strength?"

For the third time that day, the dog's tail began to wag.

CHAPTER 11

"I'm going to take him back to the clinic. Maybe I can do something, but I won't know until I get a better look," Dr. Coleman said. "Cliff, give me a hand."

While Jack whispered soft words of comfort, slowly and very gently the two men untangled and lifted the small bundle from the rails. The dog whimpered once, then was quiet. Only its eyes remained open, silently pleading.

The vet gently laid the dog onto a pile of blankets inside the Jeep. "It's going to be a bumpy ride," he warned Jack as he got in the other side, "so hold on. Here we go."

Twenty minutes later, Jack helped his father place the dog on a table in one of the examining rooms.

"Now, let's see what we've got here," Dr. Coleman said to his patient. "From the looks of you, I'd say you're some kind of terrier. Part schnauzer too."

He ran his fingers lightly over the dog's body, feeling

for broken bones, lumps or any other injuries.

His hands moved down to the legs. Two were badly mangled. What had been the left front and back right legs were now only a jumbled mass of splintered bone. They were completely useless.

Dr. Coleman worked his way back up the body. It had several nasty-looking cuts. When his fingers got to the neck, they found a deep gash about two inches long, just above a dirty cloth collar. The thin strip, black with soot, was barely noticeable. Turning it around in his hand, Dr. Coleman noticed a small rusty tag.

"Why Jack, this dog belongs to somebody. The tag says he belongs to a Fred Quimby."

Jack's heart stopped at the words. "Well, that's tough," he said sharply. "I found this dog and he's mine. I'll take real good care of him and I'm old enough anyway and you said I could get..."

His rambling was getting nowhere because already Dr. Coleman had started writing Quimby's phone number on a notepad.

Jack tried to think of something…anything…he could say to get his dad to change his mind.

"Dad! You can't! He's mine! If that man cared anything about him, he wouldn't let him get out where he could get hurt. He doesn't care about him. He's mine!!"

Jack tightened his hold on the dog, who yelped and opened its eyes.

Dr. Coleman put down the pad. "Jack, you know he's not yours. It wouldn't be right not to call this man. Suppose he's worried sick. You *know* I have to call him."

Jack could hear his father's voice in the other room. "Of course. We'll be waiting for you." Then the sound of the phone being hung up.

His eyes stung with tears. He couldn't believe his father had called the man. His dad never did anything wrong. As a matter of fact, he always seemed to know how to make everything right. But this wasn't right. How could he do this? How could his father be such a traitor? It wasn't fair.

The minute his father walked back into the room, Jack exploded. "I hate you!" he screamed before he could stop the words. "You're letting my dog go. You don't care about me. I hate you!"

He ran outside and stood by the front door and waited for a stranger to come take his dog away.

CHAPTER 12

Fred Quimby was 72 years old. All his life he had lived out in the country on Hanging Rock Creek, the same place where President Andrew Jackson witnessed his first Revolutionary War battle as a 13 year-old boy.

Quimby had grown up in a farming family, and like his father and grandfather, chose to stay where he was born and be a farmer too.

And now, more than 50 years later, he was still working his land. But even though farming was his work, hunting and fishing were still his first loves.

Since he was a boy, he would sneak off and roam the nearby fields and creeks with his dogs. And until now, there hadn't been a dog that he couldn't train...until this one, the one that some vet now had in his office.

As he drove along he thought back to the dog's first days with him. Jasper had been a gift from his son Thomas and his daughter Anna. Jasper wasn't a hunting dog like the others he'd always had, but instead a small "lap" dog, a mixture of terrier and who knew what else.

Anna insisted Jasper should stay in the house with him to keep him company. Since his wife had died earlier in the year, both his children thought a house dog would be the best thing.

Truth was, he and the dog just never were right for each other. Jasper had been a pistol right from the start. And try as he might, he just couldn't seem to control the animal. The dog was just plain untrainable. Wouldn't mind either.

To make matters worse, the dog chewed up everything. It was three days ago when Jasper's little teeth found the antique sofa in Quimby's den that the dog was banished to the yard and no longer free to enjoy the comforts of being a house dog. That's when he ran away.

And now he's turned up, more dead than alive, Fred Quimby said to himself. *What am I going to do with that dog?*

CHAPTER 13

Jack's eyes could no longer see anything but the driveway leading up to the clinic's front door. He checked his watch and saw that half an hour had passed since his father had called that man.

Maybe he won't come, he thought. *Maybe he decided the dog was too much trouble. Maybe...*

His hope vanished when he saw an old blue Chevy pickup turn into the driveway. An old man got out and approached him slowly and a little stiffly.

"My name's Quimby," he said. "Somebody called and said they found my dog Jasper. Is this the right place?"

Jack was tempted to tell the biggest lie he'd ever told, but decided it would only bring more trouble.

"Yes sir," he answered grudgingly, "that was my dad. Your dog," it hurt to say, "is inside."

Jack started to follow but changed his mind and reached over and pushed the front door open for the old man.

He was slumped down beside the door for only a few minutes when it opened again and Mr. Quimby came out, followed by his father who was carrying the dog wrapped in a blanket.

"As I told you sir," Dr. Coleman was saying, "he's in bad shape and..."

"Just put him in the truck," the old farmer interrupted, "and I'll see to him. I'll do what has to be done."

"What did he mean by that?" Jack jumped quickly to his feet and followed.

"I just don't understand this dog," the farmer continued. "He's the only one I've ever had that I couldn't do nothing with. It's a bad end for sure. But I can't say I'm surprised."

"Wait a minute!" Jack cried, looking at his father. "What's he going to do?"

"Why son," the old farmer broke in, "I'm going to take him home and shoot him."

CHAPTER 14

Shoot him! Shoot him! The words made everything around Jack move in slow motion. Jack thought it was his imagination but his father continued to move toward the old man's truck.

"Mr. Quimby, I still say it would be much better to let me do what has to be done here. It's quicker and it's pain-less."

"Where I come from, my way is just as quick and just as painless. And cheaper," Quimby added, looking directly at the veterinarian, "if you know what I mean."

Jack reached out a hand to stop his father, but his sharp look told him it was useless. He watched helplessly as his father opened the other door of the Chevy. Removing the blanket from around the dog's body, he stretched it across the seat and placed the dog on top. He and Jack watched as the old farmer settled in behind the wheel.

"Mr. Quimby," Dr. Coleman said stiffly in his most professional voice, "would you at least mind if my son says his goodbyes? He's become quite attached to *your* dog."

Quimby nodded and started the engine at the same time. Jack reached in to pat the dog's head. His throat was so dry, words wouldn't come. Instead they stuck in his throat in a white, hot clump. Tears rolled down his face. He pressed his cheek down on top of the dog's head and squeezed close.

"Sorry son, gotta get going," Quimby said impatiently. Jack whispered something in the dog's ear and pulled away. As he did, he saw it again! The little tail firmly rapped the blanket!

Before he could say anything, his father held a hand up to quiet him. "Mr. Quimby," Dr. Coleman said, "I've been thinking about what you said and you're right. I feel badly about getting you all the way out here for nothing. Besides it's my responsibility as a doctor to do the right thing for every animal I treat."

"So here's my offer. I take the dog off your hands right now." Before the farmer could protest, "And since I put you out so, I assume all costs. It won't cost you a cent."

"What's the catch?" the farmer asked suspiciously.

"No catch. The dog will be my responsibility. It saves you time and trouble. And don't forget about money."

"I'll do all the work. Fair enough?"

"You'll handle everything?" Quimby repeated. "And I won't get a bill?"

"Absolutely not. I'll even put it in writing if you want," Dr. Coleman suggested.

Quimby didn't hesitate. "No need," he said. "Take him."

CHAPTER 15

Father and son watched Quimby drive away. He never looked back.

"Some people don't..." Dr. Coleman started but cut himself short.

Jack held his bundle tighter. He could barely contain his excitement. The dog was his! But at the same time, looking at his father, he felt embarrassed.

"Uh, Dad, I uh, I'm sorry for what I said about hating you and all." He swallowed hard. "I don't. I uh, just..."

His father looked him in the eye and nodded. "I know you don't," Dr. Coleman said gently, "but I want you to remember something. Hurtful things can never be taken back once they've been said. Don't ever forget that."

He put his arm around Jack. "Now, let's take this pup inside. I've got a lot of work to do. You'd better call your mother and tell her we'll be late."

Jack was so relieved. Everything would be all right

now. His dad would fix everything and...

"I know I don't have to say this," Dr. Coleman said stopping suddenly at the door, "but I will anyway. This dog is in bad shape and not out of the woods by any means."

Jack's joy vanished like last night's rain.

"But you know I'll try. One good thing is this dog seems to be a fighter. And he's pretty brave."

Dr. Coleman gave Jack's shoulder a squeeze. "He reminds me a little of you."

CHAPTER 16

Jack handed his father the surgical instruments one by one. He knew each by name from working at the clinic on weekends.

Before starting, they both had washed their hands with a special soap to kill any germs. Then they snapped on white plastic gloves and put masks over their mouths.

First, Dr. Coleman gave the dog a shot to numb the area around its badly mangled legs so it wouldn't feel any pain.

Then, quickly and with steady hands, Dr. Coleman removed the crushed legs from the rest of the body. While he worked the dog lay perfectly still with its eyes closed.

A needle and nylon thread, just like the fishing line Jack used on his rod and reel, closed up the places where the legs had been. It reminded Jack of what the doctor did to his arm when he cut it badly falling out of a tree two years ago.

Once the legs had been taken care of, Dr. Coleman worked on the deep cuts on the body and neck. Putting some antiseptic on large cotton balls, he cleaned each one. Then the needle and thread went to work again and Dr. Coleman stepped back to have a look.

The dog still hadn't stirred.

Everything in the room was very quiet. Jack and his dad hadn't spoken to each other at all. So when he heard a strange noise coming from the dog, Jack looked at him with alarm.

"Dad what's...?" But his dad only laughed. "It's okay son," he said. "Look closer."

The dog had its eyes closed but now its mouth was open slightly. A raspy sound was coming from its mouth. He was snoring!

• • • • • • • • • • • • • • • • • • • •

"Okay, we've done our part," Dr. Coleman said as he and Jack started cleaning up. "Now we'll let him rest. He did very well."

Jack let out a big sigh, suddenly aware that he had been holding his breath. Despite what his dad said, he sure would feel better if the dog would move a little bit.

"By the way," his dad broke in, "how about a name? What are you going to call him? I heard Mr. Quimby call him Jasper. What do you think?"

Jack leaned down to put his face next to the small furry head. "Not that. He's mine now."

As he spoke, the small brown eyes opened and looked directly at him.

Then the little tail flicked, giving the metal table a small thump.

To Jack, it seemed the loudest, most glorious noise in the world. Of course! He knew exactly what to call his dog!

"Flick," he said, still nuzzling the small head. "My dog's name is Flick."

CHAPTER 17

Dr. Coleman and Jack went home that night with their news about Flick.

The Coleman family reaction was mixed. Emily was not at all sure about having a dog around. "He won't eat my fish, will he?" she asked her brother uncertainly.

"Of course not," Jack replied, rolling his eyes. "Dogs don't eat fish, you dip. Cats do," he said, smiling at his mother who was petting Fric and Frac.

Mrs. Coleman smiled back. She knew the time had come and that her boy needed a dog. To tell the truth, she wasn't quite sure who was more excited about this dog — Jack or her husband. So maybe *both* of her boys — Jack and Dr. Coleman — needed the little puppy.

Jack still couldn't believe his luck. He went to the clinic every day to be with Flick and reassure him. The anxiety that he felt after Flick's surgery lessened with each day and finally disappeared on the third day.

Six days after the surgery, he was sitting with Flick in the recovery kennel when his father walked in.

"How's our patient?" Dr. Coleman asked.

"Eating good today," Jack said, pointing at the half empty bowl.

"Glad to see that." His dad smiled. "I think it's safe to say your Flick is out of the woods. If he keeps on this way, you can take him home in a few days."

Jack had never known such joy. For the next few days, his mind was filled with just one thing. It was his first thought upon waking each morning and his last before drifting off to sleep at night.

I have a dog. My very own.

EPILOGUE

The first days of June promised another long, hot South Carolina summer. School vacation had just begun and Jack and Flick were ready.

Flick had stayed at the clinic for a little over a week. His cuts and sores healed beautifully. He was cleaned up, given a nice bath and sent to his new home exactly eight days after his surgery.

He had grown steadily over the past few months. Once Jack had gotten him home, Flick settled easily into life as a Coleman. Even Emily and Mrs. Coleman found themselves all together in love with him.

"He really is a cute little thing, isn't he?" his mother cooed.

"For Pete's sake Mom, a guy's dog isn't supposed to be cute," Jack complained. "Don't say that when any of the guys are around."

But she was right, Jack admitted to himself. Flick was something else. In the past few months he had turned out to be one great-looking dog.

Flick actually looked like several different dogs; he had a face like a schnauzer with bushy eyebrows and a moustache and a body like a terrier with long legs, floppy ears and a short tail.

He had grown another foot in length and, at almost a year old, was now almost two feet long and twelve inches high. His weight had picked up too and he was a good ten pounds. His coat, which had been so dull and dirty, was now a shiny silver and black and white.

He hardly seemed to miss those two legs at all. Despite having only one front and one back leg to walk on, he could still outrun Jack. And when they went fishing, Flick carried Jack's rod. In his mouth! He had even learned a new trick.

And Jack knew exactly who he wanted to show it to.

• • • • • • • • • • • • • • • • • • •

Clifford Washington's green Pontiac pulled into the Coleman driveway late one Thursday afternoon. Jack and Flick were the first to greet him.

"Jack, I can't get over how good that pup of yours is doing," the stationmaster said as he bent down to pat Flick's head. Flick responded with a lick and a thump of his tail.

Mr. Cliff laughed. "That tail! Still going, I see. A little faster than the last time I saw him, though. Good thing it didn't get run over when the rest of him did. It sure saved his neck that day."

"Mr. Cliff, wait'll you see!" Jack burst out. "You're not gonna believe what he can do!"

"Now hold on son," Dr. Coleman said playfully as he walked up. "Let the man catch his breath. How are you, Cliff?"

"Tingling with anticipation," Washington replied with a wink, "over the great feat which I am about to witness. So Jack, show me!"

Jack and Flick led the two men around to the side of the house where a three-foot-high split rail fence separated the Coleman yard from their next door neighbors.

"Okay," Jack said, "close your eyes for just a minute. And don't open them until I say."

When the two men had shut their eyes, Jack positioned Flick about ten feet away from the fence and walked back to join his father and Mr. Cliff.

Flick stayed right where Jack had put him and waited. "Okay Flick," Jack commanded. "Go, boy!!"

As the three watched, Flick broke into a run. When he got about a foot away from the fence, he sailed into the air and cleared the fence easily, then landed perfectly on the other side.

Clifford Washington's mouth dropped open. Jack ran over and hugged Flick around the neck. The two started rolling around on the ground.

"Why, I wouldn't have believed it if I hadn't seen it," the stationmaster said as he watched the two playmates. "Mike, how on earth did he do that with only two legs?"

"It's amazing for sure, and I can't take any credit for it," Mike Coleman replied. "I thought he was gone at least three times that first day. Flick's nothing medicine

can explain. He's got a lot of heart. It's a miracle plain and simple."

"Had to be. Speaking of that," Clifford said lowering his voice, "there's something I've been meaning to tell you about the day that Jack found Flick."

"You remember, when Jack told me what had happened," he continued, "I figured the dog was a goner so I took my pistol in case I had to put him down. But when I went to do it, the gun didn't work."

"I remember."

"Well," the stationmaster said, "what I never told you was, that night I took that pistol home to check it. I've never had any trouble with it before. Never."

The stationmaster paused and took a deep breath. "Mike, I pulled the trigger six times."

"It fired perfectly every time."

ABOUT THE AUTHOR

LYNN FLOYD WRIGHT has combined her two loves — writing and dogs — in writing her latest story, *Flick*. A native South Carolinian, she graduated with honors from Columbia College with a degree in Journalism in 1979. Her first two books, *The Prison Bird* and *Just One Blade,* have received several noteworthy honors, including placement on the South Carolina Children's Book Award consideration list. In addition to her children's writing, she has written for various regional, national and international publications. She and her husband Dave live in Columbia with their two dogs — a schnoodle named Skipper (the model for Flick) and a schnauzer named Nellie.

ABOUT THE ILLUSTRATOR

TONY WATERS has been drawing since he was old enough to hold a pencil. His first book, *The Sailor's Bride,* which he wrote and illustrated, was published in March of 1991. A graduate of Furman University in Greenville, South Carolina, he currently works with an architectural firm in Charleston and lives with his two cats on John's Island, South Carolina. This is his second collaborative effort with Lynn Floyd Wright.

ORDER OTHER BOOKS BY LYNN FLOYD WRIGHT

QUANTITY	TITLE	PRICE	TOTAL
_____	THE PRISON BIRD (hardback only)	$13.95	_____
_____	FLICK (hardback)	$13.95	_____
_____	FLICK (paperback)	$ 7.95	_____
_____	MOMMA, TELL ME A STORY (hardback)	$13.95	_____
_____	FLICK THE HERO! (hardback)	$13.95	_____
_____	FLICK THE HERO! (paperback)	$ 7.95	_____
_____	DADDY TELL ME A STORY (hardback)	$13.95	_____
_____	DADDY TELL ME A STORY (paperback)	$ 6.95	_____

SUBTOTAL _____

POSTAGE ($1.50 1st book + .50 each add'l) +_____

S.C Residents only: add 5% sales tax +_____

TOTAL $ _____

Send check/ money order payable to: **WORRYWART PUBLISHING COMPANY**
337 WHITE BIRCH CIRCLE
COLUMBIA, S.C. 29223- 3228

SHIP TO: _____

_____

_____

_____